Playground Detectives
published in 2014 by
Hardie Grant Egmont
Ground Floor, Building 1, 658 Church Street
Richmond, Victoria 3121, Australia
www.hardiegrantegmont.com.au

A CiP record for this title is available from the National Library of Australia.

Design by Stephanie Spartels

Printed in Australia by Griffin Press, an Accredited ISO AS/NZS
14001:2004 Environmental Management System printer.

1 3 5 7 9 10 8 6 4 2

The paper this book is printed on is certified against the
Forest Stewardship Council® Standards. Griffin Press holds
FSC chain of custody certification SGS-COC-005088. FSC
promotes environmentally responsible, socially beneficial
and economically viable management of the world's forests.

A Billie B MYSTERY

Playground Detectives

By Sally Rippin

Illustrated by Aki Fukuoka

hardie grant EGMONT

Chapter One

Billie B Brown sits with her
friends in their brand-new Secret
Mystery Club Headquarters.
It is a treehouse that seems to have
appeared out of nowhere, just like
magic, in the old apple tree at the
end of Billie's backyard.

One day, there was nothing in the tree but an old bird's nest. The next, there was the most brilliant treehouse Billie and her friends could ever imagine.

Billie knows it was her dad who built the treehouse. She also knows it was her dad who organised the trail of notes with secret codes, to keep them busy while he was building it.

All their parents were in on it.

2

Each of them came up with a code they knew only their child would be able to crack.

Even though the treehouse is the most wonderful surprise ever, Billie and her friends have decided it wasn't a real mystery if their parents made it up. It was more like a fun game.

But Billie has had an idea. A super-dooper idea. There is something at school she thinks the SMC should investigate.

'Please tell us, Billie!' Mika begs. 'We can't wait until tomorrow. Go on! Just give us a clue.'

'Well, all right,' Billie says, grinning, and she draws the others in close to listen. 'I guess I can tell you now. You remember how Benny got called into the principal's office last week for putting leaves in Rebecca's sandwich?'

Jack, Mika and Alex all nod.

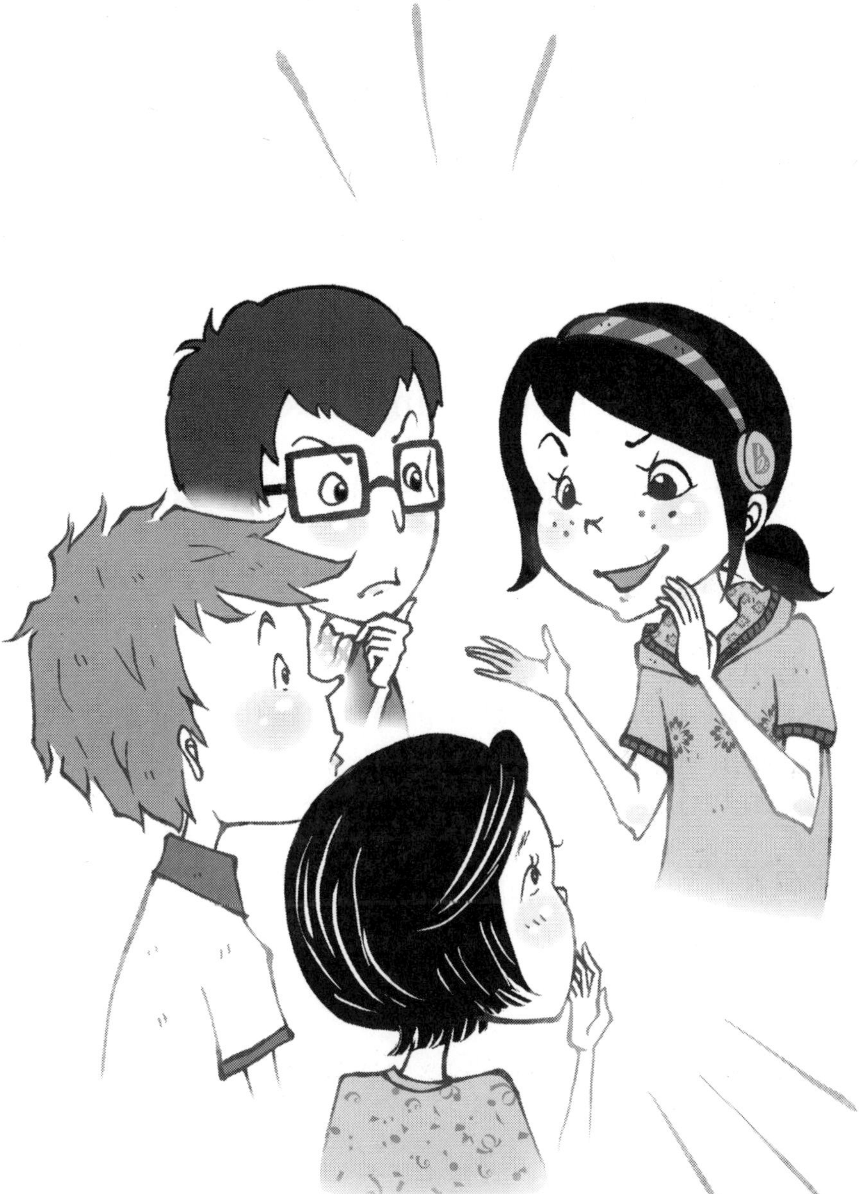

'Well, I don't think it was him,' Billie says. She crosses her arms and smiles triumphantly, waiting to see what the others will say.

'Of course it was him!' Alex snorts. 'Benny always does stupid things like that.'

'And Lola said she saw him in the corridor by the school bags that day,' Mika adds. 'When she was going to the bathroom. So there's even a witness.'

'Yes, but did she actually see him put the leaves in Rebecca's sandwich?' Billie asks. 'She's only a witness if she actually saw him do it.'

'No, but his pockets were full of mulberry leaves,' Alex says, reminding Billie. 'He was pretty much caught red-handed, Billie. Case closed.'

'Yeah, that's definitely evidence,' Jack says. 'He had leaves in his pockets, Billie!'

'Maybe,' says Billie, staring mysteriously into the distance. 'But he still says he didn't do it. He says the leaves were for his silkworms.'

'Wouldn't *you* say you didn't do it?' Alex says.

Billie shrugs. 'I might, but not Benny. He loves boasting about all the silly things he does. He thinks it makes him look cool. But this time … he seemed different.

Didn't you notice? He was almost in tears when Mr Benetto sent him to Mrs Singh's office. He kept saying, "I didn't do it! I didn't do it!" That's not like him at all.'

Mika nods slowly. 'You have a point,' she says. 'I've never seen Benny cry before. Not even that time he broke his arm at soccer.'

'It's true,' says Jack. 'But who else would put leaves in Rebecca's sandwich? It's a pretty stupid thing to do.'

A slow smile creeps over Billie's face. 'Well? Isn't this a mystery we can solve?'

'*That's* your super-dooper mystery?' Alex says, looking unimpressed. 'I thought it would be a bit more exciting than that!'

'I think it's a good idea!' Mika says, standing up for Billie. 'If someone got in trouble when it wasn't their fault, isn't it important to find out who really did it?'

'Yeah,' says Jack. 'It's not fair if Benny got in trouble for something he didn't do.'

'And now Rebecca's not talking to him,' Mika says. 'Neither is Lola.'

'What do you think?' Billie asks looking hopefully at Alex. Even though he is annoying sometimes, she still wants him to like her ideas.

'I guess you're right,' says Alex.

'Then we start our investigation tomorrow!' Billie says happily.

She sticks her hand into the middle
of their circle. Jack slaps his hand
down on hers, then Mika, then
Alex. 'Cock-a-doodle-dooooo!'
they all shout together.

Chapter Two

'Billie!' Billie's mum calls to them from the back door. She has Noah on her hip. 'Mika's mum is here to take Mika and Alex home.'

The four of them climb down out of the treehouse one by one, landing on the grass with soft thuds.

Billie looks up at the little house again and smiles. From the ground it is completely hidden by the leaves. She feels her heart almost burst with pride.

'Let's meet in the playground before school tomorrow to discuss our plan,' Billie says to the others. 'I'll bring my special secret notebook. We can write down our ideas in there.'

'Oh! I have a little digital voice recorder!' Alex says, remembering.

'If we interview people we can record what they say.'

'Good thinking, Alex!' Billie says. 'Come on, let's go inside. But remember, everyone, this is top secret – OK?'

'OK,' agree the others and they run inside.

After Billie's friends have left, Billie goes upstairs to find her dad. He is in the bathroom giving Noah a bath.

Billie's little brother is splashing about so much that her dad is covered with water and bubbles. Billie giggles when she sees him.

'So,' she says, leaning against the doorframe. 'This treehouse just appeared in our apple tree.
Out of nowhere!'

'Really?' says her dad, raising his eyebrows. 'How astonishing!'

'What house? What house?'
Noah asks.

16

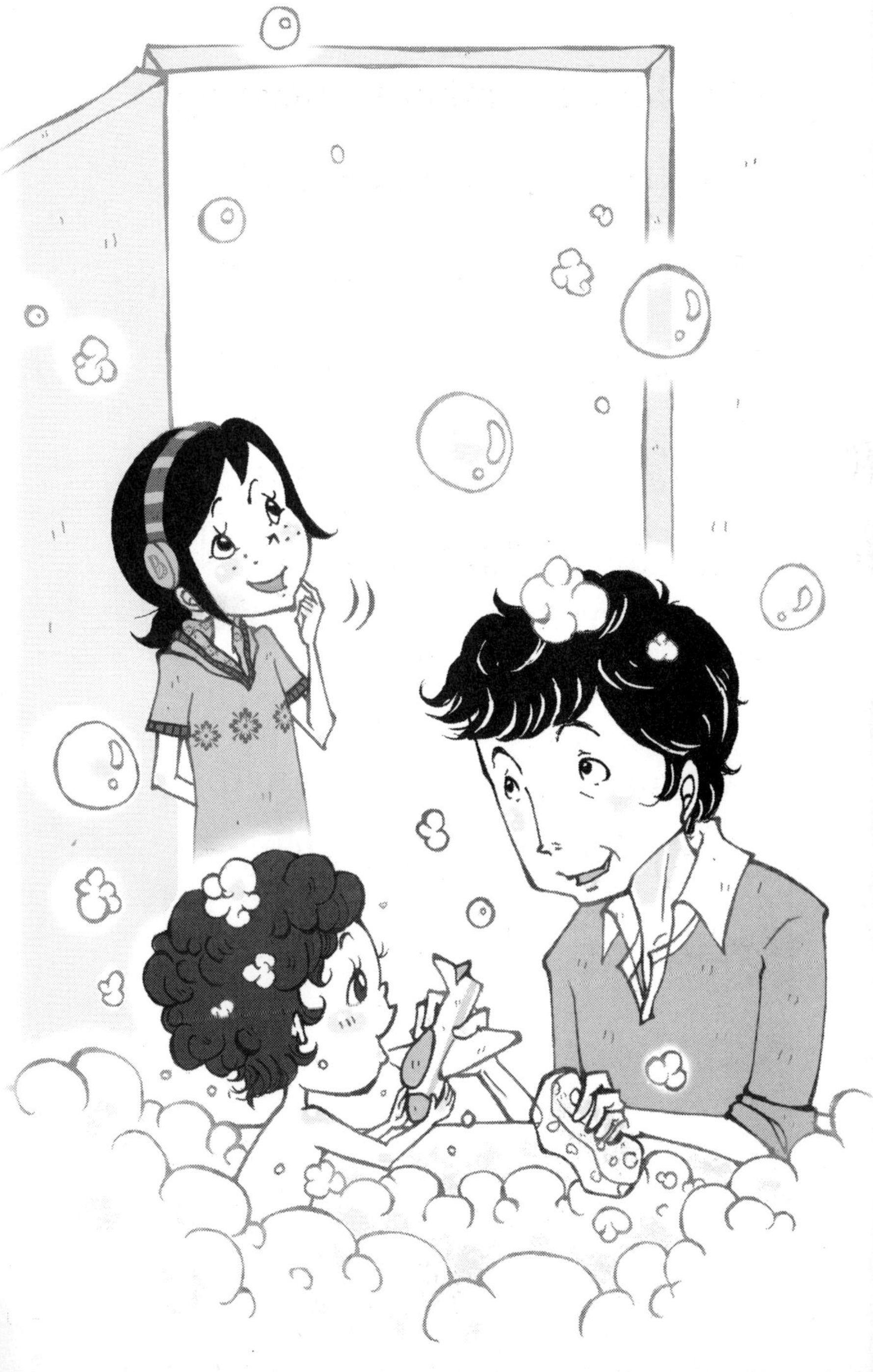

'A clubhouse. For a secret mystery club,' Billie says, grinning.

'I have no idea what Billie is talking about,' her dad says to Noah. His mouth twists up a little in the corners. 'I've never even heard of a secret mystery club. Have you, Noah? If it's a *secret* mystery club, how can I possibly know anything about it?' He winks at Billie.

'What secret? What secret?' Noah says. 'Can I have a house-club-tree-secret?'

Billie and her father laugh. Billie wipes some bubbles from her dad's cheek and gives him a big kiss. 'Thanks, Dad,' she whispers. 'You're the best.'

Her dad winks and dabs some bath foam onto her nose. 'You'd better go. Otherwise you'll get covered in bubbles, too!'

Noah squeals and tosses a fistful of foam into the air. Billie ducks away quickly and jogs back downstairs.

Yummy dinner smells are coming from the kitchen, mixing with the lovely lemony smell of the biscuits her dad baked that afternoon.

Billie pulls a stool up to the kitchen bench and perches beside her mum, who is grating carrots. 'What's for dinner?' she asks.

'Spaghetti bolognaise,' her mum answers, smiling.

'My favourite!' Billie says, happily.

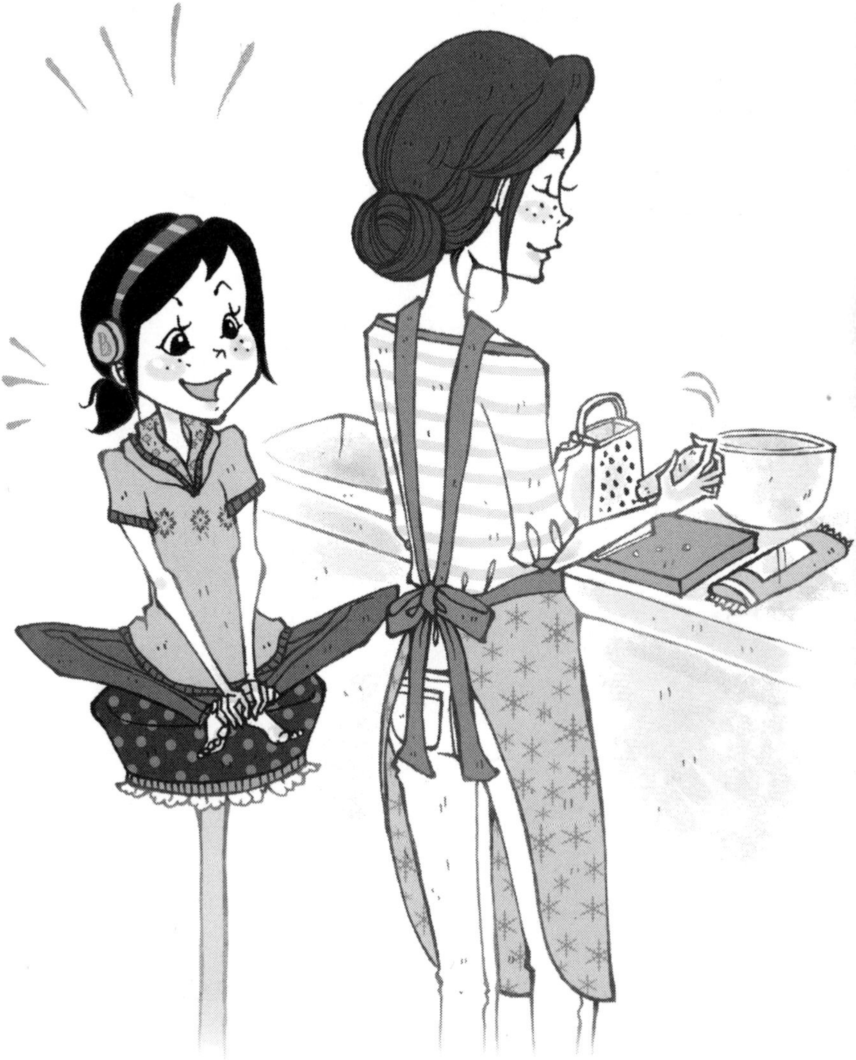

At that moment she feels like the luckiest girl in the world. She has a secret treehouse, three best friends and a new secret mystery to solve.

Chapter Three

The next morning, Billie arrives at school extra early and waits for Jack, Alex and Mika under the peppercorn tree in the playground.

She takes her notebook, which has a real lock, out of her school bag and opens it up to a clean page.

Across the top of the page she writes the date in curly writing with her blueberry-scented pen. Then she draws a wiggly line and some stars underneath for decoration.

Her notebook is so small that now almost the whole page has been filled, so she writes in extra-small writing:

SMC Mystery number 3: Who put leaves in Rebecca's sandwich?

When she looks up again, her friends are jogging towards her across the playground. They sit down beside her and look over her shoulder to read what she has written in her special secret notebook.

'So, what's the plan?' Jack asks.

'Well, I think we should start by asking people questions to find out some clues,' Billie says. 'But don't make anyone suspicious, OK?

We don't want them to know we are investigating a mystery.'

Jack, Alex and Mika nod.

'Why don't I talk to Benny?' says Billie. 'And see if I can get any more information out of him.'

'Good idea,' says Mika. 'I'll talk to Rebecca at lunchtime. We're on compost duty together today.'

'Great!' says Billie.

'I'll talk to Lola,' says Jack. 'She's the main witness!'

Alex shows Jack how to work the recorder, and the two of them record each other making funny voices. Billie and Mika giggle.

Just then the bell goes. 'Oh no,' says Billie. 'We still haven't worked out our whole plan.'

'I think we have enough to start with,' Alex says. 'Let's interview people today, then why don't we meet in the treehouse after school and we can share anything we've found out?'

'Good idea,' says Billie. 'Will your parents let you come over?'

'I think it should be fine,' says Mika. 'My mum can take Alex home again afterwards.'

'Great!' says Billie. 'Then, let's get to work. And meet you at the treehouse after school!'

The four of them run off to class.

Chapter Four

The first class for the day is art, which Billie is very happy about. Firstly because she loves art and secondly because their teacher, Ms Parkes, doesn't mind if they talk in class. It is the perfect opportunity to do some secret detective work.

'OK, kids!' Ms Parkes calls out as the students shuffle into the room and perch on stools around the big tables. 'Today we are going to work on our Saving The Environment posters to put up around the neighbourhood. Who can remember some of the topics we discussed last week?'

Lola shoots up her hand. She always likes to be first to answer questions.

'Yes, Lola?' says Ms Parkes.

'Recycling. Saving water. Not littering …' Lola says, counting the topics off on her fingers.

Ms Parkes interrupts her. 'Excellent, Lola. Anyone else?'

Billie puts up her hand. 'Not wasting electricity?' she says.

'Good,' says Ms Parkes. 'Benny?'

Benny looks up, quickly. He has been staring out the window. 'Sorry?' he says, his cheeks turning pink.

'Have you thought of a topic for your poster?' Ms Parkes asks.

Benny looks down at his desk. 'Um, not yet,' he says quietly.

'How about "Not destroying other people's things"?' Lola says, glaring at Benny.

Benny glances at Rebecca and his cheeks turn from pink to red.

'That's enough,' Ms Parkes warns Lola. 'Benny has already been punished for what he did.'

'But, I didn't …' Benny mumbles, then he stops and looks back out the window, frowning. Billie feels sorry for him.

'All right, everyone, I'd like you to work in pairs,' Ms Parkes tells the class, 'so make sure you choose someone you are going to work well with.'

Billie jumps up and walks over to Benny. He looks up at her in surprise.

Jack looks surprised, too. He and
Billie always work together.
But Billie gives him a secretive
look, which he understands straight
away. He nods and walks off to find
someone else to work with.

'Can I work with you?' Billie asks
Benny.

Benny narrows his eyes
suspiciously. 'Why?' he says.

Billie shrugs. 'Because you're
good at drawing trucks.

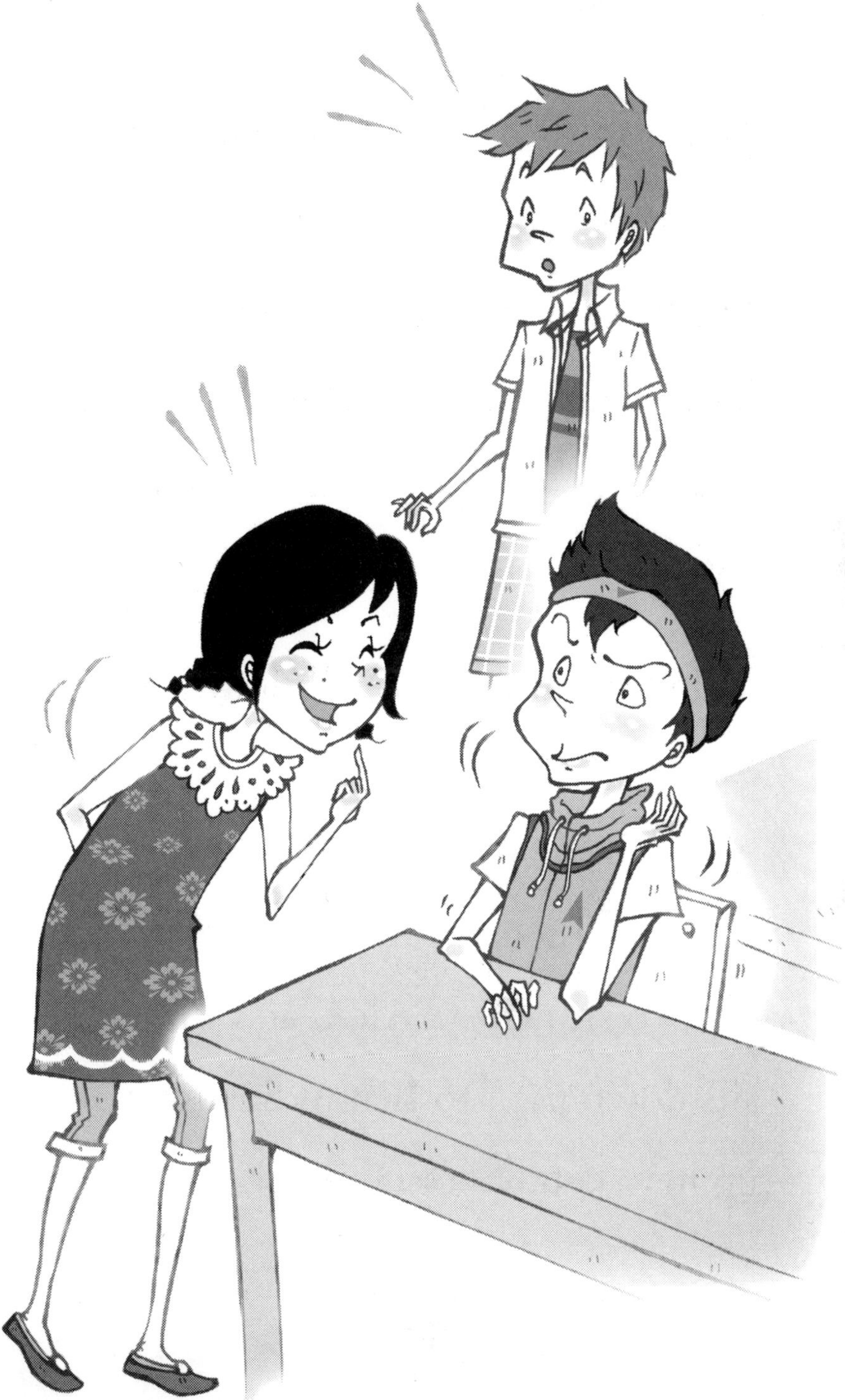

I want to do a poster on recycling, and I need someone to draw a recycling truck.'

'Well, all right,' Benny says slowly, looking pleased. 'But who's Sam going to work with?'

'I'll work with Sam,' Alex says quickly. He taps his top pocket where Billie knows he has hidden his voice recorder. So Sam walks over to sit next to Alex, and Billie sits down next to Benny. She opens up her sketchbook.

'So, I was thinking we could draw a normal rubbish truck and a recycling truck, then draw the different things that go into each of them,' Billie says. 'You know, like glass and paper and milk cartons go in the recycling truck, and plastic bags and other stuff go in the rubbish truck. What do you think?'

Benny shrugs. 'OK,' he grumbles.

'Are you still upset about what Lola said?' Billie asks. 'Why do you even care what she thinks?'

'I don't!' Benny scowls. 'It's just that everybody believes her and not me.'

'Well, you do do lots of silly things, Benny,' Billie says. 'Why should we believe you didn't do it this time?'

Benny frowns. 'I wouldn't do something like that to…' he stops. 'Never mind. Nobody believes me anyway.' He looks over to where Rebecca and Lola are sitting. When Rebecca looks up, he quickly looks away, his cheeks flaring pink again.

'Rebecca won't even talk to me anymore,' he mumbles. 'She won't even look at me! She used to be nice to me, but now…' He sighs.

Billie's brain begins to whizz. Suddenly she thinks she understands. A smile creeps over her face. 'You … like Rebecca!' she whispers slowly to Benny.

'What?' Benny says, his eyes flashing. 'Don't be silly, of course I don't! That's stupid!'

'You do!' says Billie, grinning.
'I can tell! You watch her all
the time. And you go all funny
whenever she looks at you.'

Benny looks like he might cry.
'Billie,' he begs. 'Please be quiet!
She already hates me. Don't make
it worse.'

Billie puts her hand on Benny's
arm. She has all the information
she needs. *Why would he put leaves in
Rebecca's sandwich if he likes her?* she
thinks. *That doesn't make any sense!*

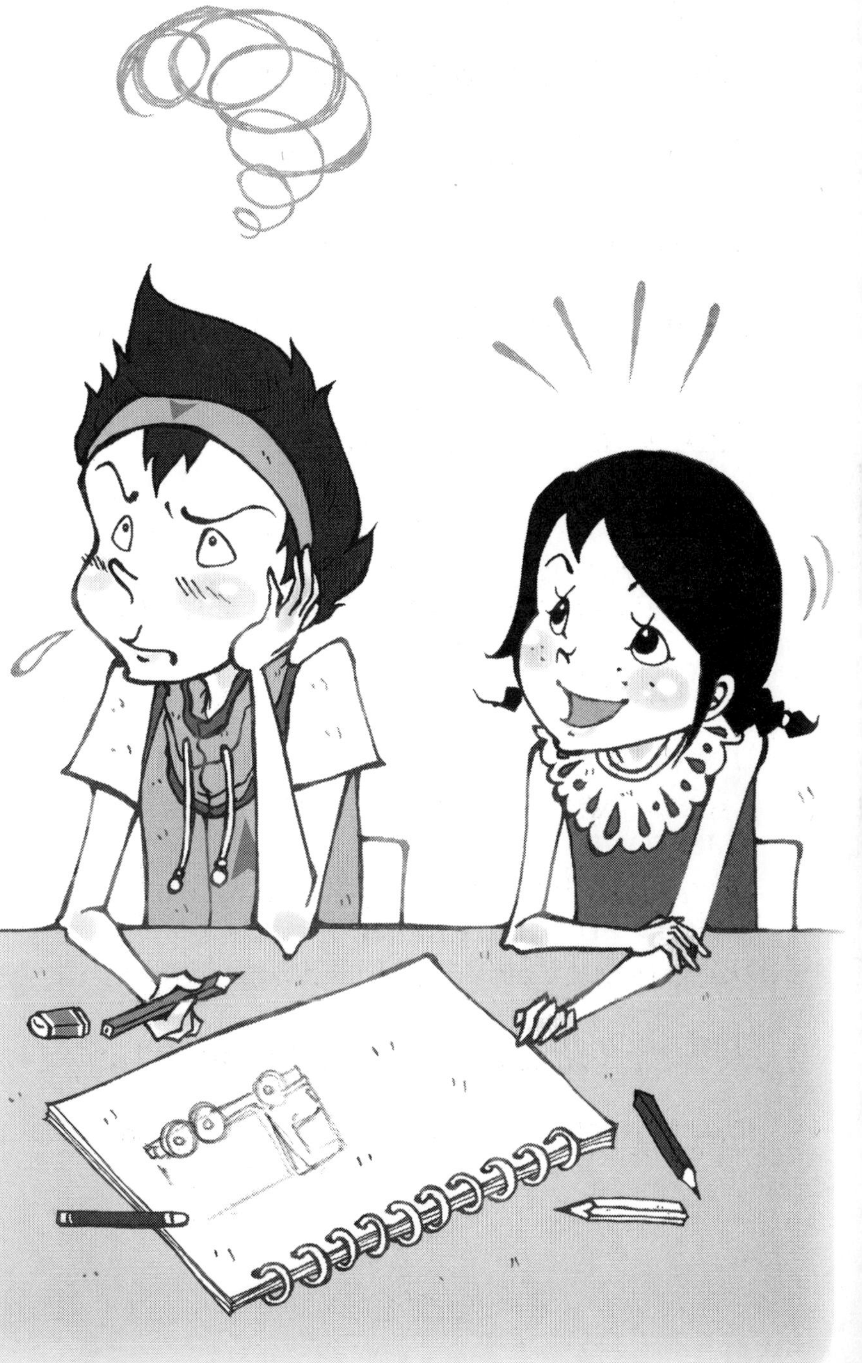

'Don't worry,' she says kindly. 'I won't tell anyone.'

Benny breathes out in relief. 'Promise?'

Billie nods. 'I promise,' she says.

Now Billie is one hundred per cent sure that Benny didn't commit the crime. She looks around the classroom. Everyone is chatting noisily about their projects.

But then if Benny didn't do it, who did? she wonders.

Chapter Five

At the end of the day, the Secret Mystery Club meet in their new clubhouse in Billie's backyard.

Billie's mum has made some snacks for them and Jack has brought over a bottle of home-made lemonade from his house.

The four of them munch on rice crackers and hummus as well as the lemon biscuits Billie's dad baked the day before.

Outside, the sun is shining fiercely, but inside the secret treehouse, high up in the apple tree, it is cool and breezy.

Billie lies back on the cushions she has borrowed from her bedroom and gazes out the window at the dancing leaves.

She thinks this could possibly be the best place in the whole wide world.

'So, back to business!' Alex says, slipping the last rice cracker into his mouth. He pulls the voice recorder out of his pocket and grins.

Billie, Mika and Jack crowd around to listen to what he has recorded. They hear Alex and Sam chatting about their poster and the noise of the class in the background.

Finally, they hear Alex ask Sam, 'Hey, you know those leaves in Rebecca's sandwich? Do you think Benny really did it?'

Then they hear Sam's voice: 'Of course! Who else would do something like that? I thought it was pretty funny, actually. It's not like Rebecca couldn't eat the sandwich once she'd pulled the leaves out. Those girls always make a big deal out of nothing.'

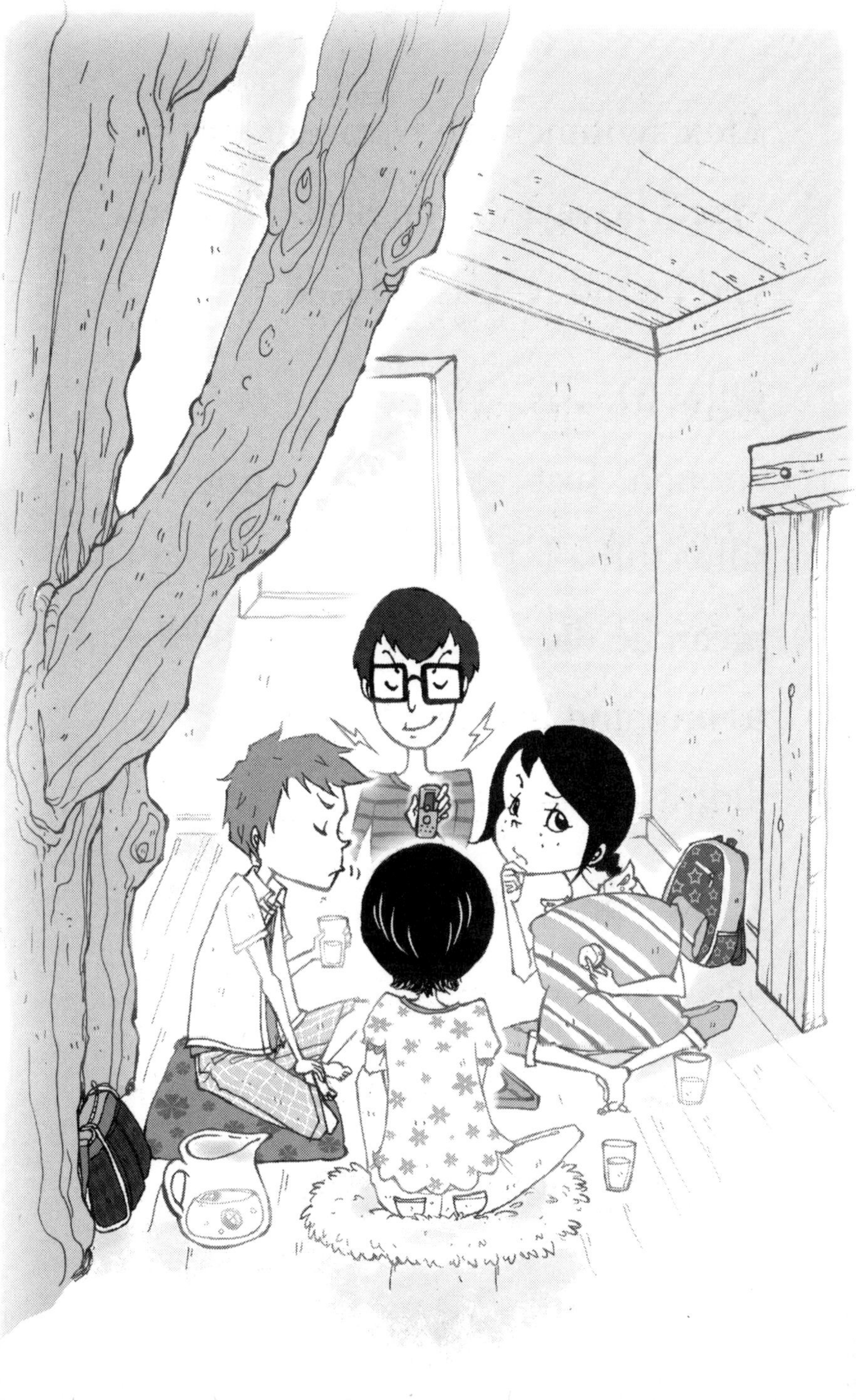

Alex switches the recorder off. 'See?' he says. 'Even his best friend said he did it. Case closed.'

Billie frowns. 'That's not good enough. Just 'cause Benny does silly stuff a lot of the time, doesn't mean he did it this time. I talked to him and I'm absolutely sure he didn't do it.'

'How come?' Mika asks. 'What did he say?'

Billie frowns. She wishes she could tell them what she knows.

But a promise is a promise. 'I can't say,' she says. 'You'll just have to trust me.'

Mika sighs. 'I have to agree with Alex on this one, Billie. Sorry. I talked to Rebecca at lunchtime. She's absolutely sure Benny did it. She says he's always staring at her. Like he's just waiting to do something horrible.'

'But that's because…' Billie stops, feeling frustrated.

Her friends look at her expectantly.

'Oh, never mind,' she mumbles.

'Jack? Did you get a chance to talk to Lola?'

'Not yet,' Jack says. 'She stayed inside at lunchtime to finish off her poster. I thought it would look a bit suspicious if I hung around to talk to her.'

'True,' says Billie. 'But I still think we should try to talk to her tomorrow.'

Jack shrugs. 'Look, even his best friend said he did it, Billie. I don't think there's really much of a mystery here. Everyone thinks it was Benny.'

'Well, I don't!' says Billie, feeling a little annoyed that her friends are giving up so easily. 'And I'm going to prove it!'

'How?' Mika asks.

'By finding out who did do it,' Billie says, crossly.

Chapter Six

That evening before dinner,
Billie takes out her secret notebook
and turns to a fresh page. On it,
she writes a list of names and puts
a tick next to the ones they have
already spoken to:

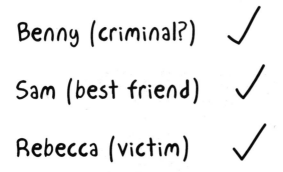

Benny (criminal?) ✓

Sam (best friend) ✓

Rebecca (victim) ✓

That only leaves one person: Lola. She's the one who told everybody it was Benny who had put the leaves in Rebecca's sandwich. She is the main witness.

'Dinner!' Billie's mum calls from the bottom of the stairs. Billie locks up her secret notebook and hides the key under her pillow.

Then she runs downstairs and sits at the table. Billie's mum is buckling Noah into his highchair. Her dad is still at the kitchen bench, finishing dinner.

'So, how was your day, Billie?' her mum says, as she cuts up Noah's food.

'Good,' Billie says, like she always does. She is too busy thinking to come up with a better answer.

'Anything else?' Billie's mum smiles.

Billie grins and tries a bit harder. 'We're doing posters in art,' she says. 'On saving the environment. We're going to put them up around the neighbourhood when they're finished. I want to ask Alf if I can put one up in his shop.'

'That sounds great!' Billie's mum says, sneaking a forkful of food into Noah's mouth. He frowns and spits it out.

'I do it!' he says crossly and grabs the fork.

Billie giggles as she watches him try to spear a piece of meat onto his fork. Finally, he just picks the food up with his hands and shoves it into his mouth.

Billie giggles as she watches him.

Just then, Billie's dad comes to the table carrying a plate of something that looks like fat green caterpillars.

'Ew!' says Billie. 'What's that?'

'Dolmades!' Billie's dad says proudly. 'I made them myself!'

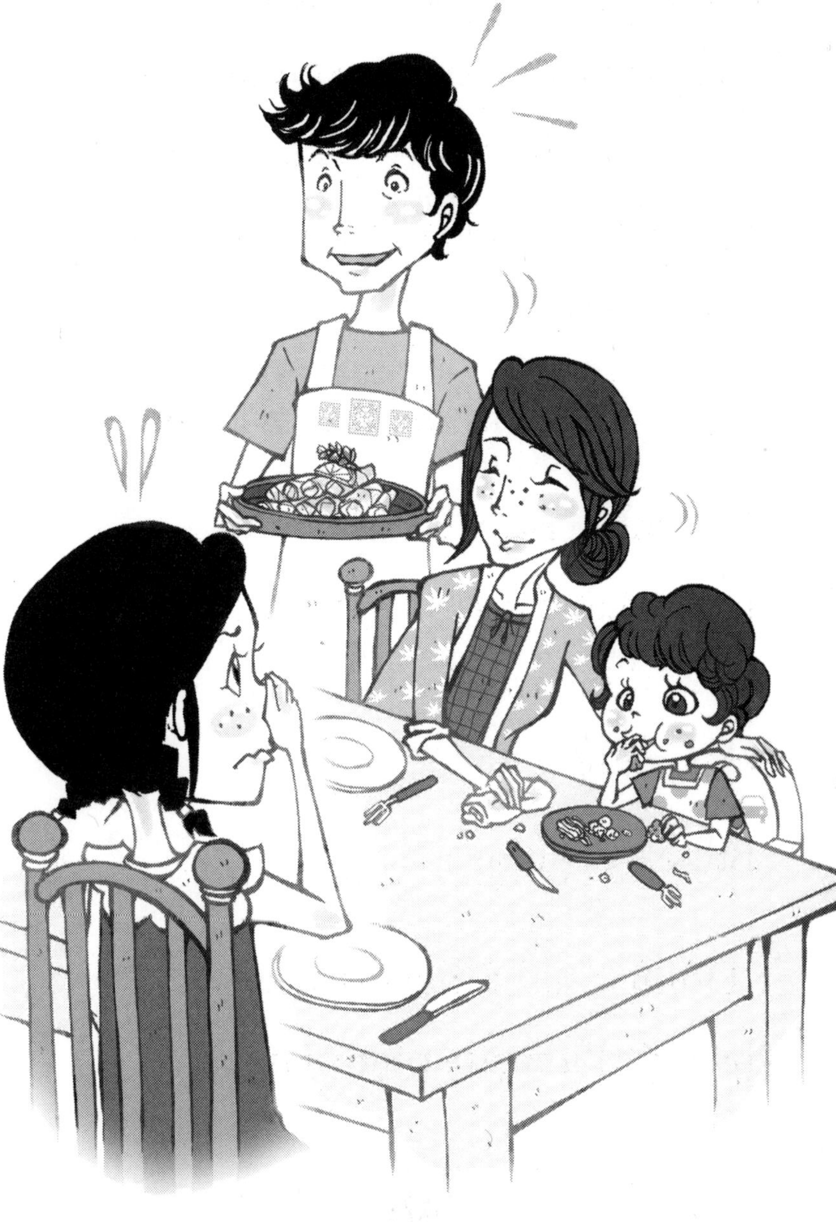

'Doll-what?' says Billie, peering at the strange food in front of her.

'Dolmades,' Billie's dad says, picking one up and putting it on Billie's plate. 'Vine leaves stuffed with minced lamb and rice. Try one. They're delicious!'

'Vine leaves?' says Billie. 'What, you mean like a grape vine?'

Billie's dad nods.

'I didn't know you could eat leaves,' Billie says, suspiciously.

She picks up the little bundle and takes a nibble. Her dad is right. It is delicious!

'Of course you can!' Billie's dad laughs. 'You can eat lots of leaves. Vine leaves, dandelion leaves, nasturtium leaves, mulberry leaves…'

'Mulberry leaves?' Billie interrupts.

Her dad nods.

'You can really eat mulberry leaves?' Billie says, chewing slowly as an idea comes into her head.

'Sure,' says her dad. 'I probably wouldn't eat them raw, but they're not poisonous, like gum leaves or rhubarb leaves are.'

'So…' says Billie. 'Gum leaves are poisonous, but not mulberry leaves?'

'Uh huh,' says Billie's dad, putting another couple of dolmades onto Billie's plate.

But Billie is deep in thought.
She has discovered another clue!

Chapter Seven

The next day at school Billie waits until the afternoon to talk to Lola when her class has sport. She hasn't stopped thinking about the mystery and the new clues she has uncovered, but it is like her friends have forgotten all about it!

This week Billie's class is playing dodgeball. Billie knows that Lola is good at ballet, but she is terrible at dodgeball.

Just as Billie expected, Lola is the first person to get hit by the ball and has to sit out. Billie is quick to make her move. She sees the ball coming her way and jumps in front of it so it hits her in the legs.

'Billie's out!' someone shouts.

Jack looks over at her in disbelief.

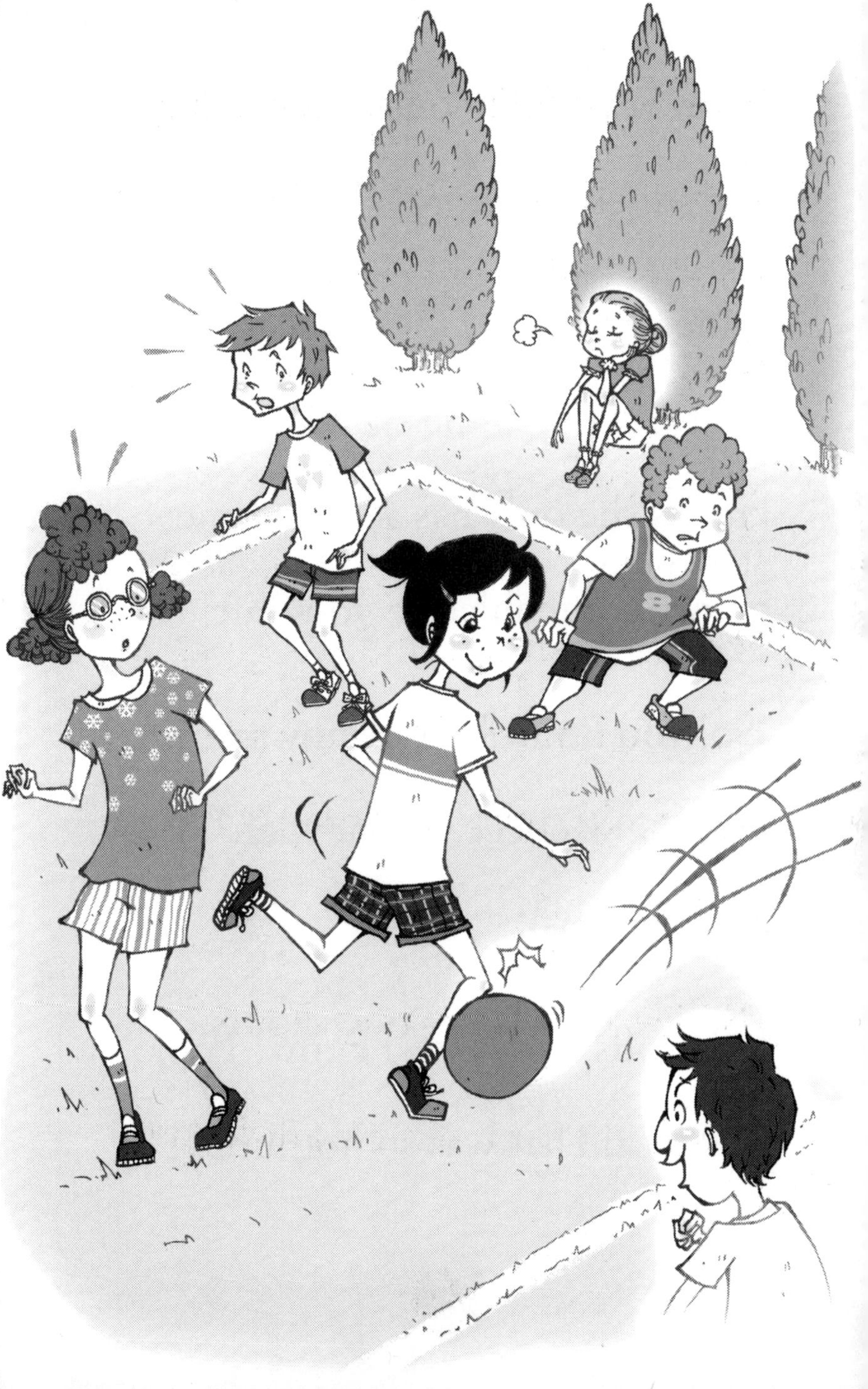

Billie has never gone out so quickly in dodgeball before!

Billie shrugs and jogs over to sit next to Lola in the shade. She knows she only has a short time before someone else goes out.

'So, you know how Benny put leaves in Rebecca's sandwich?' Billie begins.

Lola rolls her eyes. 'I know! Poor Rebecca. That was so not funny!'

'But they were only mulberry leaves, weren't they?' Billie says. 'It's not like they were poisonous, like gum leaves. She could have still eaten her sandwich if she picked them out.'

'No, they were gum leaves!' Lola says, frowning. 'Poor Rebecca had to throw her sandwich out and she had nothing for lunch that day. I had to give her some of my sandwich – or she would have starved!'

Lola talks very quickly and doesn't quite look at Billie as she is talking. Suddenly Billie has a thought. She needs to be very careful, though.

'But didn't Benny have mulberry leaves in his pocket?' she says. 'He said he was taking them home to feed his silkworms.'

Billie watches Lola's cheeks turn red.

'Maybe they were mulberry leaves then!' Lola says quickly.

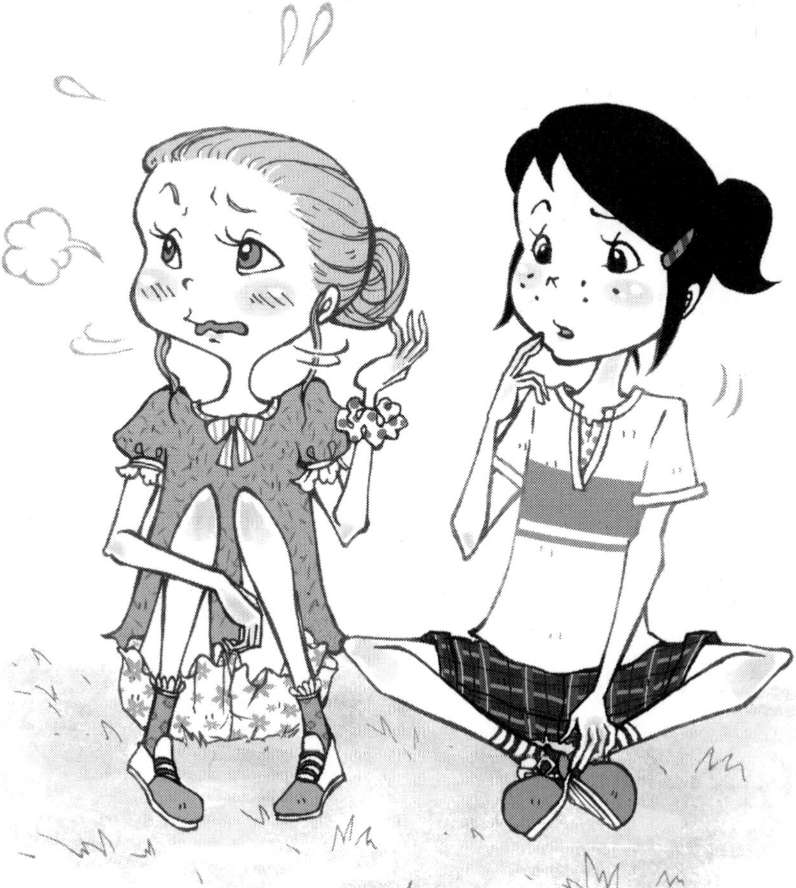

'How should I know? It's not like I saw them close up. I only saw him from a distance when I was on my way to get a drink.'

'Putting the leaves into Rebecca's sandwich?' Billie asks calmly.

'Yes!' says Lola.

'But you said you didn't actually see him put them in,' Billie says. 'You said you just saw him in the corridor.'

'That's what I meant!' says Lola.

She looks flustered and angry. 'But he obviously did it, even if I didn't see him. I mean that's exactly the kind of silly thing Benny would do.'

'It *is* the kind of silly thing Benny would do, that's true,' Billie says, looking over at the dodgeball court where Benny and Sam are jumping around pretending to be monkeys. 'But I don't think Benny did it.'

'Of course he did!' says Lola. 'Who else could have done it?'

Billie looks back at Lola, straight into her eyes. 'I think you did it, Lola,' Billie says.

She knows that if she is wrong this is a terrible thing for her to say. But she has a very strong hunch she might be right.

Lola stares at Billie with her mouth open. Then her eyes fill with tears.

'It was only a game,' she sobs. 'It was supposed to be funny. I didn't know gum leaves were poisonous!

Rebecca put them down the back of my T-shirt when we were in the playground so I put them in her sandwich as a joke. I thought she'd think it was funny. I couldn't believe it when she got so cross!'

Lola looks desperately at Billie. 'I was scared I'd get into trouble, Billie. I've never been sent to Mrs Singh's office before.' Lola's eyes drop to the ground. 'Benny gets sent there all the time. I didn't think he'd get so upset about it.'

'Well, he got into trouble for something he didn't do, Lola,' Billie says frowning. 'I know Benny can be silly and annoying, but that's no reason for him to be punished when he's not to blame!'

Lola hangs her head. 'I guess so,' she says quietly. 'It's just that I feel like I've made such a mess now. I don't know how to fix it.'

'Yes, you do,' says Billie, folding her arms across her chest.

Lola looks up at Billie with terror in her eyes. 'You mean go and tell Mrs Singh?' she says. 'I can't do that! She'll be so cross with me for lying. I've never got in trouble with Mrs Singh before.'

Billie feels her heart soften a little when she sees how scared Lola looks.

'I'll come with you if you like,' she says kindly. 'Don't worry, I've been before. It's not that bad.'

'And believe me, you'll feel better after telling the truth,' Billie adds.

'Really? You'll come with me?' says Lola, grabbing Billie's hand. 'Thank you!'

Billie nods. 'On one condition,' she says. 'There's someone else you need to talk to first.'

Lola sighs. She look over to where Benny is loping around the dodgeball court like a gorilla and giggles. 'I guess he is kind of funny sometimes, isn't he?' she says.

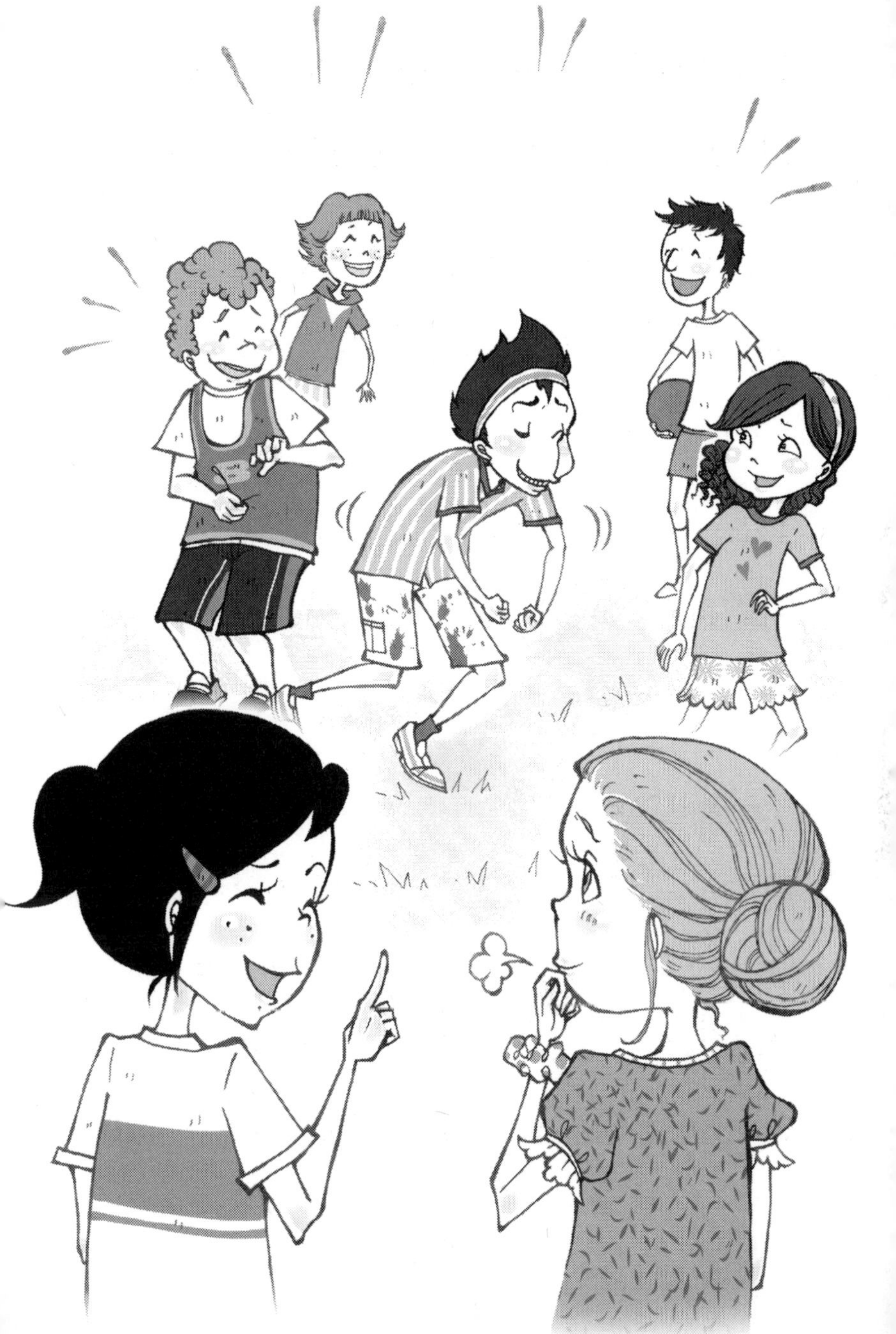

Chapter Eight

Billie and Lola wait until Mr Benetto blows his whistle to signal that the game is over. Billie nudges Lola.

'Now?' says Lola.

'Now,' Billie says. 'Before it's too late.'

Already the class is heading back to the classroom to pick up their schoolbags before they go home.

Lola takes a deep breath. Then she jogs up alongside Benny who is walking back to class on his own.

Billie watches from the shade of the peppercorn tree. She can't hear what they are saying but she can guess how Benny is feeling by the look on his face. First he looks furious. Then he looks annoyed.

Last of all he shrugs and a slow smile creeps across his face.
The two of them shake hands and Lola comes running back to Billie.

'Ready to go and see Mrs Singh?' Billie says.

Lola nods and the two of them run across the playground together.

That afternoon, the Secret Mystery Club meet up in their treehouse in Billie's backyard.

They are bubbling with excitement.

'So, mystery number three is solved!' Billie announces proudly, drawing a big cross over the page in her little secret notebook.

'I can't believe you worked out it was Lola!' Jack says, grinning.

'And you even got her to confess!' Alex adds.

'Yeah, Billie, how did you work it out?' Mika says.

Billie takes a sip of her lemonade and leans back on the cushions. Jack passes her the plate of lamingtons he has brought with him and she takes one. She chews slowly. She is secretly enjoying the attention.

'Well,' she begins, 'like I said, I knew after talking to Benny that it wasn't him, so I just had to find out who it was. Lola was the only other person in the corridor that day, so it had to be her.'

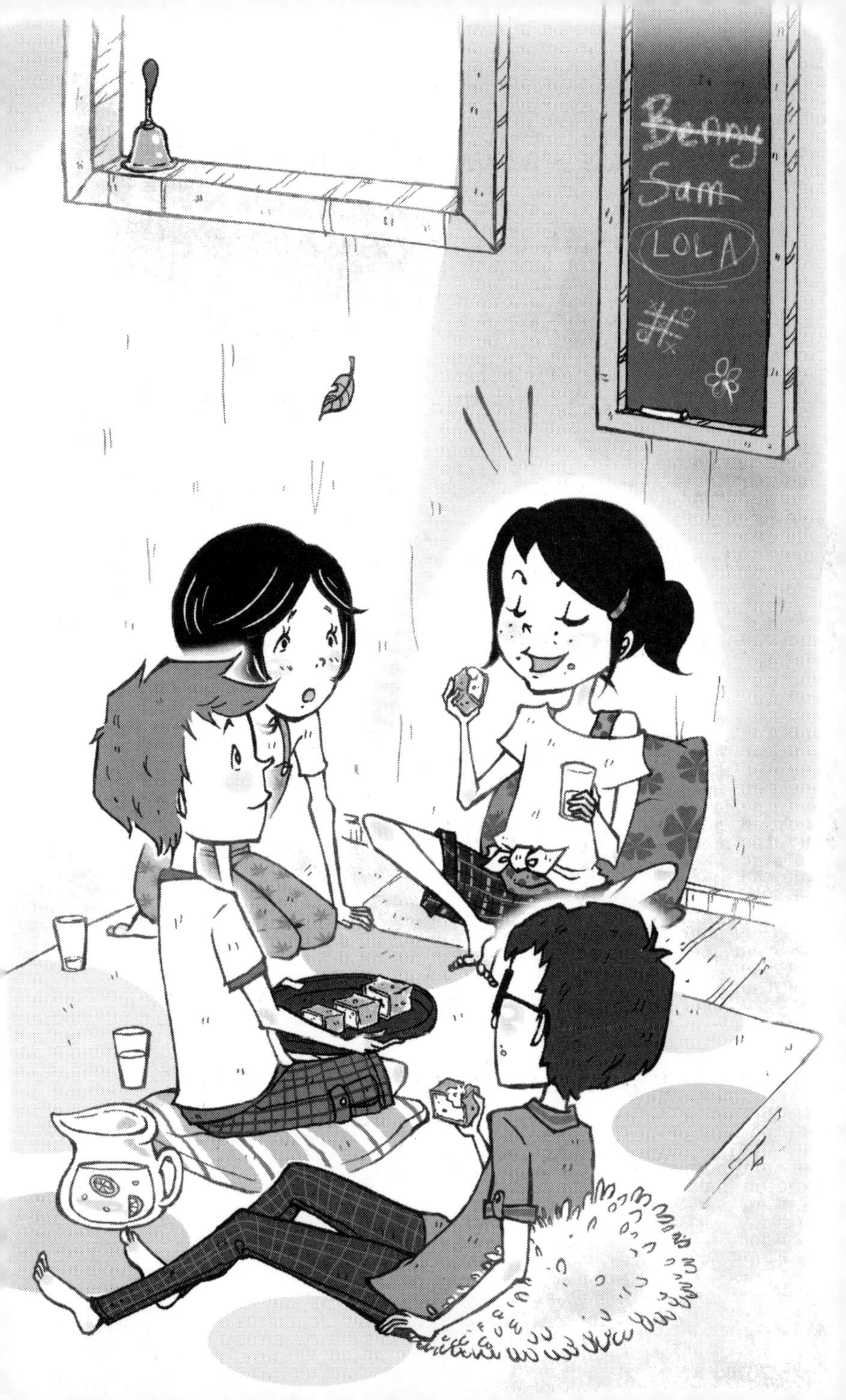
Benny
Sam
LOLA

'But how did you know it wasn't Benny?' Alex insists.

Billie brushes the bits of coconut off her lap. A bird flutters in from a nearby branch and quickly gobbles them up. 'I can't say,' Billie says. 'I promised him I wouldn't tell.'

'But we're your best friends.' Jack frowns. 'You can tell us.'

Billie shakes her head. 'A promise is a promise.'

Alex reaches for another lamington. 'So what happened when Lola went to Mrs Singh's office?' he says.

'Mrs Singh said that as long as Lola apologised to Rebecca and Benny she wouldn't be punished because it was her first time,' Billie says, rolling her eyes. 'Can you believe it? Last time I was sent to Mrs Singh's office I had to pick up rubbish all lunchtime!'

'I remember that!' Jack laughs.

Billie grins. 'In fact Mrs Singh said
Lola was very brave to come and
tell the truth – like it was her idea!'
she snorts.

'Anyway, it all ended well,'
Mika says. 'Thanks to you, Billie!'

Billie smiles. 'Thanks Mika,'
she says, feeling very proud.
'Oh, and also, Rebecca felt bad for
not speaking to Benny all week.

So I said that maybe she should
work with him in art instead
of me. You know, to make it up
to him.'

'Poor Benny!' says Alex. 'I thought
he'd at least be allowed to work
with Sam again!'

Billie flicks the last little bit of
coconut off her lap. 'Oh, I don't
think he'll mind that much,'
she says, smiling mysteriously.

'Kids! Mika's mum's here,' calls Billie's mum from the back door. The four of them gather up the remains of their after-school picnic and climb down out of the tree.

As they head inside, Billie thinks about her day. She feels proud to have solved an extra tricky mystery — and almost all by herself!

But now what? She wonders how long they will have to wait for their next mystery.

Mrs Okinawa is talking to Billie's mum at the back door. She looks very distressed. 'My beautiful garden!' she is saying. 'All that work and now they're all gone!'

Mika runs up to her mum and talks to her quickly in Japanese.

'What happened?' Billie asks her mum.

'Someone – or something – has been stealing Mrs Okinawa's strawberries,' Billie's mum says.

89

'I said it was probably the birds, but she says that she had covered the whole strawberry patch with netting. It's very strange. The netting wasn't even touched, but nearly all the strawberries are gone.'

'Oh no,' says Billie. 'That's terrible!' She knows how much Mika and her mum love their garden.

Billie's mum shakes her head. 'I wish I had an answer – but it's a mystery to me!'

Billie feels a little shiver of excitement pass through her.

She looks at Jack, Mika and Alex.

By the smiles on their faces, she can see they are thinking the same thing.

The Secret Mystery Club has another mystery to solve!

To be continued...

A BillieB
MYSTERY

The Secret Mystery Club's next

mystery might be their trickiest yet.

Who is stealing Mika's strawberries?

Find out in
*Strawberry
Thief*